W9-AKE-009

# WHERE'S CHIMPY?

**BERNIECE RABE**

*Photographs by Diane Schmidt*

**Albert Whitman & Company**     **Niles, Illinois**

*To Misty Spurlock* B.R.
*For Lee Balterman,*
  *and with special thanks to my mother, Miriam Schmidt,*
  *and Terri Hoffman* D.S.

Library of Congress Cataloging-in-Publication Data
Rabe, Berniece.
   Where's Chimpy?
   Summary: Text and photographs show Misty, a
little girl with Down syndrome, and her father
reviewing her day's activities in their search
for her stuffed monkey.
   [1.   Down syndrome—Fiction.   2.   Mentally
handicapped—Fiction.   3.   Lost and found possessions—
Fiction]   I.   Schmidt, Diane, ill.   II.   Title.
PZ7.R105Wg   1988        [E]        87-37259
ISBN 0-8075-8928-4   (lib. bdg.)

*Text © 1988 by Berniece Rabe*
*Photographs © 1988 by Diane Schmidt*
*Design by Karen Yops*

Published in 1988 by Albert Whitman & Company, Niles, Illinois
Published simultaneously in Canada
by General Publishing, Limited, Toronto
10 9 8 7 6 5 4 3 2 1

## About Down syndrome

Down syndrome is a chromosomal disorder which usually causes mental retardation and certain physical characteristics. The exact cause and prevention are currently unknown.

Although the risk of having a child with Down syndrome increases with a woman's age, women under thirty-five give birth to more than eighty percent of children with Down syndrome. The incidence of Down syndrome is approximately one in every eight hundred live births; one quarter million families in our country are affected.

There is wide variation in mental abilities, behavior, and physical development in children with Down syndrome. But all are children with the same dignity and rights as their "normal" peers. Children with Down syndrome deserve to live full lives. Good, loving families; mainstreamed educational, recreational, and work experiences; and positive public awareness—all can help children with Down syndrome be the best they can be.

Diane M. Crutcher, Executive Director
National Down Syndrome Congress

It was time for bed.
    "Snuggle in, and I'll read you a story," Daddy told Misty.

But Misty didn't want to listen to a story. "I want Chimpy," she told Daddy. She couldn't go to sleep without her toy monkey.

Daddy looked around Misty's bedroom. "I don't see Chimpy. Where is he?"

"I don't know," Misty said. She looked under the covers. She looked under the bed. "Chimpy gone."

"You can find Chimpy tomorrow, my tired little girl,"
Daddy said. "Right now you need to go to sleep."

"I want Chimpy," Misty said.

"All right," said Daddy. "Then we'll have to find him." He
took off his glasses. "Where were you and Chimpy playing
today? Think hard!"

Misty thought and thought. She remembered she had
played with her friends on the swing set. She had let Chimpy
swing a time or two by himself.

It was easy for Daddy and Misty to look for Chimpy because it was still light outside.

Chimpy wasn't by the swing set. But Misty did find her Joseph Doll and Happy Clown there.

"I want Chimpy," Misty told Daddy.

"Let's try the car," Daddy said. "Remember you took
Chimpy when you rode to Grandma's today?"

Misty remembered. She had taken Chimpy in the car.
He'd wanted to see Grandma, too.

When Misty looked in the car, Chimpy wasn't there. But she was glad to find her pink purse on the front seat.

"Where's Chimpy?" she asked Daddy.

"This calls for more hard thinking," Daddy said. "Where else have you been?"

Again, Misty thought hard. "In the den," she told Daddy. She remembered she had played with Kitty and Chimpy there.

"That's it!" Daddy said. "Go find Kitty, and you'll find
Chimpy."

Misty went to the den. Chimpy was not near the chair
where Kitty liked to sleep.

But she did find her blue ball.

Misty kept looking. She checked the dining room — under
the table and chairs. She found her Mother Goose book.

She looked on the sofa in the living room. There was her necklace.

She went outside again and searched through her basket
of blocks. Many-Colored Rabbit was there. But not Chimpy.

Daddy picked up all Misty's toys with one arm and Misty
with the other. "Just this one night you'll have to go to sleep
without Chimpy."

"No way!" Misty told him. "I want Chimpy."

"Okay! Maybe we'd both better look. Shall we try the
sandbox?"

"Yep!" said Misty.

Misty remembered that after lunch she and her friends
had played a game with Chimpy in the sandbox. They'd
covered him up, then brushed the sand away. Each time,
they'd found Chimpy—just where they'd put him.

But now when she and Daddy looked through the sand, there was no little toy monkey. They did uncover her ditch digger.

Misty got all sandy.

"Well," said Daddy, "guess who needs a bath and a clean nightgown?"

A bath! Misty remembered something very important. She
had already taken a bath, right before dinner.

"Misty take bath. Not Chimpy. Chimpy wait. I make
Chimpy wait!"

Now Misty knew just what had happened. Before her bath
she had sat Chimpy on the pink chair in the bathroom and
told him, "Honey, wait."

Was he still there?

Misty ran to the pink chair. A towel was on it.

She pulled the towel away.

There was Chimpy!

"Chimpy on chair!" Misty said, laughing.

"Right!" said Daddy. "Chimpy was on the chair all the time. Just because he was covered up doesn't mean he was gone."

Misty picked up Chimpy and kissed him. "Sorry, Chimpy," she said.

Misty had a fast bath while Chimpy sat right on the edge of the tub.

Daddy helped Misty dry herself.

Then Misty snuggled Chimpy in her arms, and Daddy snuggled both Misty and Chimpy in *his* arms and marched them to bed.

Misty tucked in Chimpy and said, "Night-night, Chimpy honey." Then she told Daddy, "Now read story."

Daddy gave a big sigh. "Just a short story, Misty — it's getting pretty late." He reached on top of his head for his glasses. "Where are my glasses? Misty, help me find my glasses!"

Misty giggled. "Where have you been?" she asked Daddy. "Think hard!"

And while Daddy was thinking, Misty lifted up the
storybook that had dropped to the floor. There were Daddy's
glasses, right underneath!

After Daddy had finished the story, Misty looked at all the
things she had found. Joseph Doll. Happy Clown. Her pink
purse. The blue ball. The Mother Goose book. Her necklace.
Many-Colored Rabbit. The ditch digger. Daddy's glasses.

One, two, three, four, five, six, seven, eight, nine.

And Chimpy made ten.
Close your eyes, too, Chimpy honey.

J. Malan Heslop

## About Berniece Rabe

One day BERNIECE RABE looked out her window to see her neighbor playing with his daughter, Misty, who has Down syndrome. Berniece called her editor and declared, "I must do a story about Misty and her daddy—a story other children with Down syndrome can identify with. I want her to have the lead role, not the secondary role usually allocated to children with this handicap. I want Misty to be the *star*. Every child has the right to be a star sometimes!"

Berniece Rabe is the author of several other books for children, two of which star a handicapped child. *The Balancing Girl* was an ALA Notable Book and a Child Study Association Children's Book of the Year.

Lee Balterman

## About Diane Schmidt

DIANE SCHMIDT is a photojournalist living in Chicago. Her work has been published in many national and international magazines and books, including the books *Abstract Relations* and *The Chicago Exhibition*. She has been interviewed on national TV and radio programs and is the 1987 recipient of an Arts Midwest/National Endowment for the Arts grant. Recently, she has especially enjoyed taking photographs of Misty and her father for this book.

Diane has a niece named Sarah who is five and a dog named Emily who is ten. The three of them like to go for long walks together along Lake Michigan.